MELTING THE TRAPPER'S HEART

THE BRIDES OF SIOUX FALLS

INDIANA WAKE

BELLE FIFFER

JOIN MY NEWSLETTER

INTRODUCTION

Welcome to this amazing new series of romances from bestselling authors Indiana Wake and Belle Fiffer.

In this series we follow Doctor James Waters and see how he helps the women who have come to him in need. Each book is a complete story and can be read alone and in any order.

Doctor Water has got himself a new post out in Sioux Falls, South Dakota, but he has a dilemma. His neighbour, Karla Barker, has just given birth and her husband was killed in a mugging before she found out she was pregnant. Now having given birth to a baby boy Stuart, Karla is suffering. No man will marry her with the burns on her face and her son in tow. She is in dire straits, and James feels he cannot leave her behind.

Having discovered that women are in short supply out West he decides to take her with him and to see if someone will have her for a wife. Through his profession he knows of other women in similar circumstance. Through no fault of their own they have children of their own or from relatives and have no husband to help them.

Once James has this idea, he decides to take them West as mail-order brides.

The women are dubious, but five of them decide they have little hope and that this could be the new beginning they have been hoping for.

If you missed the other books grab them now

The Baby and the Burned Bride

The Bride, the Boys, and the Bank Robber

The Sheriff and the Troubled Bride

Melting the Trapper's Heart

The Bride on the Run

FREE with Kindle Unlimited.

CHAPTER ONE

The twinge in Lianne's side caught her unawares. She gasped and pressed her hand to her swollen belly. It wasn't the first twinge she had experienced, but it was getting stronger. That concerned her, even with Doctor Waters assuring her that the baby was growing nicely and not showing any signs of wanting to arrive anytime soon.

She simply couldn't lose this child. Not another one. Lianne didn't think she could go through another loss. Lance certainly couldn't. Things had been tense between them when he had left for his tour of duty. Lianne hadn't heard from him in months and now her concern had turned into suspicion mixed with a

1

pang of fear. Was he running away? Had he found an excuse to run and not have to deal with it anymore?

Lianne still missed him, though. A lot.

Ignoring the tightness in her side, Lianne finished making her bed and left her room, heading toward the stairs. Being seven months pregnant, she had been told to take things easy and not do anything to make it stressful for herself. Lianne had simply rolled her eyes at that, but her landlady had been most insistent. Beth Waters meant well, Lianne knew, but it didn't stop her frustration.

She didn't like people telling her what to do. Even her parents had been driven to despair. Lance had tolerated it, but even he had had his limits. Even with the disagreements, their love had been strong, or at least she thought, until the losses over the years had started to stretch it thin.

Lianne just wished Lance would appear and tell her he was fine, then things would be all right. She just didn't want to be alone, handling this pregnancy, without him.

Wandering into the dining room for breakfast,

Lianne was nearly at her chair when she felt another sharp twinge. This one had her buckling over and she clutched onto a nearby chair.

"Ouch!"

Instantly, a young woman was at her side, easing her into the chair.

"Lianne?" She knelt before her, brushing her hair out of her eyes. "What is it?"

Lianne gritted her teeth and waited a moment. She held up her hand when the woman tried to speak again, signaling her to wait. The twinge eased and went away. Lianne let out a slow breath of relief.

"I'm fine. It's just twinges."

Beth Waters frowned.

"From the look of it, they're quite painful. You don't think you're going into labor, are you? James said that could be a sign of early labor."

Lianne hoped not. She had been having these twinges for the last few weeks, but she had been putting it down to stress. Stress of being alone, not knowing where her husband was, being out in the middle of somewhere that was practically another world when compared to Ohio. Sioux Falls was lovely, and Lianne liked the people there, but it was a culture shock compared to what she had grown up in.

Going into labor when Lance wasn't about? She didn't want to think about that. She gave Beth a reassuring smile.

"It's not unusual, don't worry. This baby's just a massive wriggler."

"Baby?" Beth raised her eyebrows. "Are you sure it's just one baby in there?"

"I won't know until the birth, but Doctor Waters thinks it's only one." Lianne shuddered. "I hope it's only one."

Beth laughed. She gave Lianne's belly an affectionate rub.

"Well, Mister or Missy, you'd better not give your mama a hard time when you arrive. Rather you than me doing this, Lianne. I don't think I could handle giving birth to a person."

Lianne giggled.

"From what I've been told, it's not that bad." She looked at Beth curiously. "Don't you want children in the future? You could still have them."

"Haven't found the right man to have children with." Beth shrugged. "It's not a big deal. I can handle it if I don't. Looking after young mothers or widows with children makes up for it."

Even as she said it, Lianne could feel the thin veil of sadness behind the woman's eyes. Beth was a warm, loving person who did everything in her power to help. She was so much like her brother, James. Beth deserved a little happiness and Lianne couldn't believe completely that Beth was happy just looking after those with children.

"You, Beth, are such a liar," Lianne accused.

Beth's face went red. She cleared her throat and stood, brushing down her skirts.

"And so are you," she shot back.

"What do you mean?"

"All isn't well with you, Lianne, no matter how much you try to hide it."

Lianne blinked.

"I didn't think I was hiding it."

"More than you care to admit."

Lianne sighed. She picked at the stitches on her skirt, absently rubbing her belly.

"I'm just nervous, that's all. Giving birth for the first time is one thing, but doing it alone..."

She didn't need to say more. Both James and Beth knew of the situation. James had been her doctor since shortly after the first loss and he knew of everything she had been through. Lianne found her doctor to be a good confidant. So was Beth. They knew how scared Lianne was about her husband's whereabouts. No one had heard anything about him, whether he was alive or dead, which would worry anyone who knew him -- least of all his pregnant wife. Lance had been assigned to a nearby army post, but they had written to her saying Lance had gone into battle and they couldn't account for him.

He could be out there in a mass grave or wounded and wandering. It made Lianne feel helpless.

Beth reached out and squeezed her shoulder.

"You'll find out about your husband soon," she assured Lianne gently. "Don't fret."

"But I don't know what to do now, Beth. The army has no idea where he is, none of the hospitals in the area know who he is, and nobody seems to have any idea if a soldier's come through."

The knowledge there was nothing to say where Lance had gone was worrying. Lianne could only hope that he was alive and living somewhere, missing in action. Even if he had deserted the army, he would be alive.

"There is always Richard Baxendale," Beth said slowly.

Lianne looked up.

"Who's that?"

"He's a tracker who lives just outside Sioux Falls. One of the best, from what James has told me."

Lianne had heard the name before. And very recently. Then she remembered him. He had been at Simone's wedding the month before. He hadn't interacted with many people, if any, but Lianne remembered him.

7

She remembered him very well.

"Wasn't he the one who found Sheriff Dickinson's ex-wife and children?"

"Yes. He used to be in the army himself." Beth spread her hands. "You never know, he might have known Lance. He served at the same post for a period of time. You could try to recruit him, if you want."

Lianne wasn't sure about that. The first sight of Richard Baxendale across the hall at Simone and Keith Dickinson's wedding reception had been like a sucker punch to the gut. Her heart had fluttered and Lianne had felt light-headed. Roughly attractive, she had found the man to be very imposing. Lianne had never reacted to anyone like that, not even her husband.

And that made her feel awful. She shouldn't be finding another man attractive, not when she was married. That was just morally wrong.

It would be best to steer clear of him, but Lianne couldn't exactly say that to Beth. She floundered a little.

"Simone told me he was a bit gruff," she said lamely. "Brusque even."

Beth laughed.

"Aren't all men? If Simone could get him to do what she needed, I'm sure you can. And you're more tenacious that she is."

Lianne wasn't about to argue about that. But she wasn't sure if that made her feel any better. Beth smiled and urged her to sit at the table.

"Come on, have some breakfast and go find him. Ask him about Lance. You never know, he might have the answers you need."

Lianne could only hope so. Because, right now, that was practically her only option.

CHAPTER TWO

*R*ichard was happy being on his own. He didn't want anyone to bother him; it was better that way. No one was going to upset him, betray him. Richard only had himself to rely on.

What he didn't like was people coming up to his house and bothering him with tasks that drove Richard mad. He had been in the army, and he had been good at his job, but that had left him with a lot of problems. No one wanted a man who suffered from waking flashbacks in their lives. It was best if everyone stayed away.

And now, in the space of two months, he had had several visitors. Mostly Simone Dickinson and her husband, either together or separately. Richard actually didn't mind Simone and Keith was understanding of his behavior, so he allowed them into his life. But whenever anyone else came by and tried to interact with him, Richard turned them away. He couldn't be dealing with more than he had to.

Which was why he wasn't happy when he saw a raven-haired beauty who was very heavily pregnant coming up the path to his front door. From his position around the side of the cabin, standing by the pile of wood he had been chopping, Richard watched her warily. He had seen her before at Simone's wedding, one of her friends. And he had been struck by her beauty. Pregnancy suited her. Even from where he was standing, though, he could see the worry strain around her eyes. She was scared of something.

He had also seen the wedding ring. That made her off-limits; full stop. Interaction with her could be misconstrued, and while Richard didn't care what people thought, he didn't want to find himself dealing with an irate husband. It was preferable to stay away.

If only she could get the message. She had her hands pressed to her swollen belly, apprehension on her face as she approached his front door. Richard picked up his axe and carried on chopping the wood he had collected that morning. He was in his shirt sleeves, unbuttoned to show off his vest, but he was in no mood to get himself dressed appropriately. This was his private land and he wasn't getting tidied up for someone who wasn't invited.

Even as he swung the axe, Richard was aware of the woman watching him. She had followed the sounds. Out of the corner of his eye, Richard saw her openly staring at him. Her mouth was open, and her cheeks were flushed red. Richard knew he had to look a sight, covered in sweat and dressed as he was. But he wasn't changing to make her feel better. She was on his land and she would have to put up with it.

If she didn't like it, she could leave.

"Are you Richard Baxendale?"

Richard lowered the axe, wiping the sweat from his face as he glowered at her.

"Who wants to know?"

She bit her lip, her cheeks flushing more. Why did that have to make her more attractive?

"My...my name's Lianne Colebrook. Mrs. Lianne Colebrook."

Richard snorted.

"You don't need to tell me you're married, Mrs. Colebrook." He held up his hand and wagged his ring finger. "I do have eyes."

"Oh." Lianne swallowed. "I... I was told you might be able to help me."

"I highly doubt it."

"You don't even know what I'm going to ask."

Richard sighed and turned away, picking up the axe again.

"You want me to search for someone. The one who is the father of your child." He swung and split the piece of wood neatly in two. "I'm not getting involved in that."

"You helped my friend, Simone Cartwright."

"I helped her, yes."

Richard still wasn't entirely sure why. Simone had somehow got through to him. He wasn't about to do that again.

"Then you can't help me?" Lianne faltered.

"No." Richard tossed the wood pieces onto the big pile beside him. "If the father of your child doesn't want to know, then leave him be."

He started to reach for another hunk of wood. Hopefully, that was enough to shock the woman into leaving. The next thing Richard knew, the wood was being kicked out of his hand, a foot connecting with his fingers. Then Lianne was right in front of him, slapping him. Hard. Her sudden speed was enough for Richard to take a step back. He hadn't seen her move. Lianne squared up to him, breathing heavily with her eyes blazing.

She looked lovely even when she was angry. Richard shoved that aside.

"How dare you," she hissed. "How very dare you?" She jabbed a finger at his chest. "I am not a harlot. I am a married woman, and I am looking for my husband. I haven't heard from him in four months. He's in the army, and he was stationed nearby Sioux Falls shortly before I found out I was pregnant. I want to find him." She lowered her hand and stepped back. Suddenly, she looked exhausted. "Is that too much to ask?"

Richard was silent. It wasn't too much to ask at all. She just wanted to be reunited with the father of her baby. He wasn't a father, but he could imagine how frightening it was to go through something possibly life-threatening on your own.

That part he had done far too many times.

Then realization began to sink in. Richard could feel the knot building in his stomach.

"Did you say your name was Colebrook?"

"Yes."

"And your husband...was his name Lance?"

Lianne's eyes widened.

"You...you know him? You know where he is?"

She really didn't know. Richard didn't want to do this. He really didn't want to. But Lianne was not going to go away; she needed to know. Squaring his shoulders, he put the axe aside and beckoned for Lianne to follow him.

"Come with me. We're going for a little walk."

"What? He's been here all this time?" Lianne was now looking indignant. "Why hasn't he contacted me? Why didn't you? Surely, you knew he was married."

"Mrs. Colebrook..." Richard didn't know what to say. Words would not come. He swallowed. "Just...come with me. It's best you see where your husband is."

"Why can't you just tell me?" Lianne demanded.

But Richard was already heading towards the back of the house. He knew he should wait for Lianne -- a pregnant woman shouldn't be out in this heat, and it wasn't the easiest of places to walk -- but Richard didn't want to talk to her. Not until she knew the truth.

He could hear her footsteps hurrying behind him,

but Richard didn't turn around. He didn't want to see her face when she realized what was going on.

"Where is he?" Lianne caught up with him as they rounded the back of the house. She grabbed his arm. "Stop being so cryptic, Mr. Baxendale! Where's my husband?"

Richard braced himself. Then he pointed.

"He's over there."

There was a tree just beyond the back porch. It had been there since Richard had moved in. The trunk was massive, and the leaves spread out to provide welcoming shade from the sun. It was a quiet place to be.

Now it was a final resting place. Richard knew the moment Lianne saw the wooden cross he had erected under the tree. Her annoyance died away, her face turning so white Richard thought she was going to faint. As he reached for her, Lianne stumbled towards the tree. The mound where Richard had covered the body and the grave was still there, only now less prominent. It was becoming part of the scenery.

Lianne sank to her knees before the grave. A little sob came from her as Richard approached.

"Oh, God," she whispered. "Lance."

Richard knew there was nothing he could say that would make her feel any better. The shock was settling in by now, along with disbelief. Lianne wouldn't be able to comprehend that she was a widow, and had been for some months.

He hovered a little further back, unsure of what to do. He had seen men die, far too many times, but Richard had never had to deal with the aftermath. He had never had to break the news to any family members that a loved one was dead.

Lianne was shaking, her shoulders trembling. She sounded like she was trying to stop the tears. But as she spoke, he heard the emotions choking her.

"When...when did he die?"

"Four months ago." Richard wished someone else was doing this. "He came to my home badly wounded. I managed to patch him up but...he was too sick. Something that neither I or the doctor could deal with. He was too far gone by the time the doctor looked him over." Richard tried to stop himself from rambling, but he couldn't help himself. "He just...he wasn't strong enough to fight it."

"So, he died shortly before I came out here?"

"Within weeks." Richard winced. He shouldn't have said that. "He did mention you to me many times, but he never told me how to get hold of you."

"You should have found out!"

Lianne suddenly jumped to her feet. She charged at him, slamming into Richard like a rampaging bull. Richard staggered and nearly fell over, managing to catch himself before he landed on his behind on the ground. Lianne was punching him, hitting his chest and stomach. One punch caught Richard in the face, hard enough to make his teeth rattle. But Richard held onto her, cradling Lianne as she attacked him with pained screams.

Soon, the fight went out of her and she sagged to her knees. Still holding onto her, Richard lowered her to the ground and sat with her. This was awkward. He hadn't done something like this before, and it felt incredibly odd. But Richard couldn't bring himself to find a way out of the situation, not when Lianne started to wail into his arms. Her whole body was shaking, her hands now clutching onto him instead of fighting him.

Richard rocked her gently. He didn't know what else to say. Anything would have been redundant at this point.

He just felt like a complete cad.

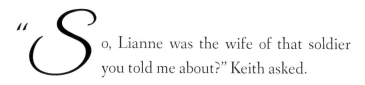 o, Lianne was the wife of that soldier you told me about?" Keith asked.

Richard nodded grimly.

"Yeah. I had to show her Lance Colebrook's grave."

Keith sat back with a whistle. They were sitting in Richard's cabin, the fire roaring nearby as they sat at the only table in the space. Their card game was practically forgotten as Richard told his friend about Lianne's visit earlier on and the shock of finding out she was now a widow. It wasn't something Richard was about to forget.

He didn't want to be in that situation again.

"How did she take it?"

Richard scowled.

"How do you think?"

Keith grunted.

"Fine. Stupid question." He began to gather up the cards. "Where is she now?"

"I took her back to the boarding house. She was in no fit state to do anything else." Richard sipped at his whiskey. "Beth Waters is looking after her. She promised that she wouldn't leave Lianne alone."

That had been some comfort. Richard didn't know why. He wasn't emotionally invested in any of this. All he had done was try to help a fellow soldier recover from his wounds. If Lance hadn't been as sick as he was, he would have pulled through. Richard had survived injuries like that before. But he had been too far gone, and Richard hadn't been able to do anything except watch as Lance deteriorated. Even the doctor had no idea what to do.

Watching someone die was something Richard could still not get used to. It just added to the nightmares he already had.

"You're still feeling guilty about it, aren't you?"

Richard frowned.

"Why would I feel guilty about anything? I didn't do anything wrong."

"Are you sure about that?"

Richard wished Keith didn't know him so well. Even after so long of not speaking to each other due to Richard's self-induced solitude, the sheriff hadn't forgotten how to read people.

"I feel guilty that I didn't try hard enough to make Lance better. I know there was nothing I could do, but that doesn't stop me feeling like that." He grimaced. "And I feel awful that she had to find out like that."

"Is that all it is?"

Keith gave him a knowing look. Richard didn't like it when he did that. It was infuriating. Keith was supposed to be in his honeymoon period, but the sheriff spent time with Richard every week since Richard had helped find his ex-wife and children.

Richard didn't know if this was Keith's way of

repaying him, and, frankly, he didn't want the thanks. But he did appreciate the company. It was during these times Richard realized how much he missed it.

"Don't talk in riddles, Keith," Richard groaned. "I'm not in the mood for it."

"Sorry." But Keith's expression said he wasn't sorry in the least. "You find her tugging at your heartstrings, don't you?"

"What heart?"

"There's a heart in there, Richard. Or you wouldn't have helped Simone to find Megan for me." Keith pointed out. "And you wouldn't have looked after Lance Colebrook."

"It's a human thing to do."

"Not with you, and I know you."

"More's the pity."

Keith ignored that.

"In a short space of time, you've helped two women when you vowed not to get involved with them again."

Richard gritted his teeth. He was beginning to wish that Keith didn't know everything before Richard had retreated from the rest of the town. It wasn't easy keeping secrets from the one person who knew everything.

"I must be getting old."

"Yes, that must be it."

Richard glared. Keith was up to something, and Richard had a pretty good idea what he was trying to do. He didn't like it. Not at all.

"You're not trying to match me to Lianne Colebrook, are you?"

"No, of course not." But Keith was still smirking. "I wouldn't do such a thing."

"Good. Because we don't need more matchmakers in Sioux Falls. One meddling in our business is bad enough."

"Doctor Waters isn't that bad."

"He may not be, but I don't want to get involved with being matched to one of the women he's brought along. Besides, Lianne only found out she was a widow a few hours ago. It's hardly conventional or sympathetic, is it?"

Keith shrugged.

"I think the period of mourning differs greatly over here."

Richard growled. The sheriff was not going to give up on that. Somehow, he had got it into his head that Richard and Lianne would be a good couple. Lianne was only coming to terms that she had lost her husband, and Richard didn't want a wife. He just wanted to be left alone.

"Sheriff, would you stop?"

"All right, I'll stop." Keith shuffled the cards and began to deal them out again. "But have a think about it. You never know; you might be surprised."

Richard would be surprised if he gave into this at all. And he had already thought about it; he wasn't going to get involved with any woman. Not now, not ever.

Why did that feel like a lie even to himself?

CHAPTER FOUR

*L*ianne was struggling. Lance was dead. He hadn't been ignoring her, because he had been buried. At the very least he had been given a proper burial.

But that didn't make Lianne feel any better. She was going to give birth soon and Lance wouldn't be there with her. Doctor Waters would be there, at least, along with the local midwife, but no husband or family.

She sat on the back porch, a blanket tucked around her lap and looked out over the back yard. It had been a week since Lianne had found out about her husband's death, and it was only just starting to really sink in. This felt like a bad dream. Lianne had come out to Sioux Falls looking for answers, and now she had them. They were just answers she didn't want.

She had to figure out what she was going to do. Lianne had left everything behind in Ohio. Her parents could take her back in, but she didn't want to impose. They were struggling as it was and Lianne didn't want to add herself and a newborn to that stress.

She knew that she would have to stay in Sioux Falls. Lianne had her friends from the boarding house and in the town, but there was only so much she could ask of them. She would have to handle a lot of it on her own.

And Lianne didn't like the thought of that.

"Mrs. Colebrook?"

Lianne looked up. And then stared. Richard Baxendale was standing near the porch, looking like he would rather be anywhere else. She hadn't seen him since he had walked her back to the boarding house the week before. In spite of his initial treatment of her, he had been very kind. Lianne had been taken aback by his sudden change of heart but had been too distraught at the time to question it. From the way he had been around her, Richard hadn't been too comfortable with it, either.

Now he stood before her, shuffling nervously from foot to foot. He looked to have had a shave recently and his clothes were a lot less bedraggled than when she had seen him last. At least he had chosen to dress more appropriately for a walk in the town, but even then, Lianne could still make out his sinewy frame against the line of the cloth. The man distracted her beyond belief, and it drove Lianne mad.

She was supposed to be in mourning, not thinking about another man. That was wrong, surely.

"Mr. Baxendale." Lianne cleared her throat, nervously smoothing the blanket over her lap. "Forgive me if I don't stand up."

"I'm not complaining."

That *was* certainly new. Lianne looked up at him. Somehow, sitting before him made her feel vulnerable.

"What are you doing here?"

"I... I wanted to see how you were doing." Richard

looked rather sheepish. "See if there was anything I could do."

He didn't need to. He could have just walked away and not have any further contact with her. Lianne was touched. She gave him a small smile.

"Nothing at the moment, Mr. Baxendale," she said. "But thank you for the offer."

Richard nodded. He looked like he wanted to leave, but he made no attempt to walk away. Lianne had not seen a man look so close to near jumping out of his skin. Was she the reason he was uncomfortable? Lianne didn't think she was capable of doing that to anyone -- especially in her current state.

"I..." Richard cleared his throat, his cheeks flushing. "Do you mind if I sit with you for a moment?"

He didn't want to be here, but Lianne wanted to be selfish for a moment. She shrugged.

"I don't mind."

Richard hesitated a moment more, and then he settled onto the porch steps just in front of her. He put his Stetson on the floor beside him, absently running his hands through his hair. He looked sweet when he was nervous. Softer, even. Lianne didn't think, with the brief moments she had been in his company, that Richard had the ability to be soft. It was a side of him that she found she liked to see.

It was a pity that Richard was so out of sorts.

"How are you feeling today?" he asked, looking up at her with those haunted eyes. They had snagged Lianne right at the start, and she couldn't bring herself to look away.

"A little numb." Lianne absently rubbed her belly. The baby was wriggling around like mad. "Confused. I've done a lot of crying, but I don't think it's really sunk in."

Richard nodded. He rested back against the porch post.

"I'm so very sorry I wasn't able to get hold of you at the time. It's just…"

"Don't be sorry. It's happened now. I just need to move past it."

Lianne wasn't angry at him anymore. Things had got out of hand, and it wouldn't have been the top priority on the list. She understood that now. After calming down and having time to think, Lianne realized that Richard had done everything he could at the time. She couldn't be angry at him for trying to help her husband.

"How long had you been married?" Richard asked.

Lianne looked down at her wedding ring, still on her finger. She couldn't bring herself to take it off.

"Four years. We had wanted to start a family as soon as possible, but..." She bit her lip. "I wasn't able to keep the babies."

"You mean you had miscarriages."

Lianne nodded.

"Far too many to count. My body just wasn't capable of keeping them to full term." She laid a hand on her belly. "This pregnancy is the first time I've managed to keep it past six months."

From what Doctor Waters had told her, a baby could be born after six months, but it was preferable to wait as long as possible. The baby had less chance of surviving, the sooner it was born before full term. Lianne didn't want to go through more heartbreak.

"And now you don't have a husband in your life," Richard murmured.

"No." Lianne swallowed back the hard lump in her throat. "It's not what I wanted for life, but I have to put up with it."

She wanted her husband back. Raising a baby alone wasn't what she had wanted out of her life. Lianne understood the risks Lance had taken by being a soldier, but he had been taken far too young. She recalled she had told him about the pregnancy in one of her letters and his response had been joyful. She could tell he couldn't wait to finally be a father.

Now that would never happen.

"If you need any help, just let me know," Richard said. "It's the least I can do, seeing as I messed up the first time around."

"You didn't mess up. You didn't know about it."

Richard grunted. He was looking less uncomfortable than he had been a few moments ago. His presence wasn't as unnerving as Lianne thought it would be. It was...nice.

They sat in silence for a time. As they watched the

scenery and world go on around them, Lianne found herself glancing over at Richard. The silence wasn't awkward at all. Richard was the type of man who spoke when he had something to say and Lianne liked that about him. She didn't feel the need to fill up the empty space with conversation. Everyone else around her wanted to talk, it seemed, which steadily became infuriating. There were times when it was perfectly appropriate to be quiet and soak up the surroundings.

Just like now.

His profile wasn't too bad to look at, either. Thin and angular with a solid jaw and thick black hair, Richard was certainly an impressive man. But Lianne could see the haunted expression, the tiredness in his eyes. Something kept him up at nights. And it must plague him even when he was awake.

Lianne knew about the stories of soldiers having nightmares from their time on duty. Was Richard one of them?

"May I ask you a question, Mr. Baxendale?" she asked.

"You may." Richard glanced up at her with a lopsided smile. "And it's just Richard. Mr. Baxendale makes me feel far too old."

"Richard." Lianne smiled back. "As long as you call me Lianne. I can't exactly call myself Mrs. Colebrook anymore."

"Fair enough." Richard rolled his shoulders. "What's the question?"

"You look like you're gearing yourself up."

"I don't know if I will like the question."

Lianne laughed.

"You are a strange man."

"I've known that for years." Richard gestured with his hands. "Come on. What's the question?"

"Why did you help Simone look for Keith's ex-wife?"

Richard sighed.

"I've been asking me that myself. All I can come up with is Sheriff Dickinson is an old friend. I suppose I just wanted to help him."

"Even with your attitude?"

"Attitude?"

"You're very standoffish with a lot of people." Lianne pointed out. "You keep yourself apart as much as you can."

Richard arched an eyebrow.

"I didn't realize you'd kept me under observation."

"I am an observant person. And it's just my opinion on what I've seen."

Richard grunted.

"I like my solitude. Is there anything wrong with that?"

"No, not at all. I was just curious about why you like to be alone."

"Because I want to be." Richard gave her a hard look. "Women are far too curious for their own good."

"Is that a general observation or about someone specific?"

"Specific with regards to you, yes. It's my business, Mrs. Colebrook."

He was keeping himself at an arm's length. Lianne could see the invisible walls going up. She sighed.

"Sorry. I just wanted to know more. You're not exactly someone who is easy to read."

"And I like to keep it that way." Then Richard closed his eyes and let out a heavy sigh. "I'm sorry. That was harsh. It's not your fault."

Lianne wasn't offended. She had already come to her own conclusions about him. Solitude had nothing to do with his former life as a soldier. It was something far more personal.

"Somebody hurt you badly, didn't they?"

Richard growled and looked away. His expression said everything.

"Who was she?" Lianne pressed gently. "Your wife?"

For a moment, she didn't think Richard would answer her. When he did speak, it made Lianne jump.

"I was engaged once. When I was a little younger than you. Beatrice and I were going to be married after I'd spent a year in the army, saving up for the wedding. Two months in and she wrote to me, saying that she didn't want to be married to a soldier and she was now married to someone else."

Lianne stared. She had expected a woman to have hurt Richard before -- a woman could make a man be in more pain than he cared to admit -- but nothing so callous. Now she could understand his attitude and how he kept himself away from everyone.

"I... I'm so sorry."

"Don't be," Richard said sharply. "It's in the past."

"It may be the past for you, but it clearly still hurts."

Richard growled and looked away.

"I should have kept my big mouth shut."

"You don't like being under scrutiny, do you?"

"Not really." Richard snorted. "And I don't like being closely watched."

Lianne smiled.

"Lance found it a frustration as well. But he liked that I was honest. You need honesty in your life at times. No lies, nothing."

"Sounds like he was a good man," Richard murmured.

"He was."

They sat in silence for a moment longer. Then Richard rubbed the back of his neck, now looking sheepish.

"I'm not the best person you want around, but if you need anyone to talk to, you know where to find me. I may not be a good conversationalist, but I am a good listener."

Lianne was touched. She smiled.

"Thank you."

The smile she got in return was enough to have her heart skipping a few beats. When he relaxed, Richard Baxendale had such a handsome smile.

CHAPTER FIVE

*I*t was hard at the beginning to cope with the knowledge that she was a widow, and that Lianne would be giving birth and raising a baby alone. Over the next two weeks, it was easier to get up and get on with her day. The tears weren't as intense as before, and Lianne began to feel anger and frustration towards Lance. How dare he leave her like this? How dare he die? It was all irrational, but Lianne couldn't stop herself from thinking it.

She did her best to occupy her time. Beth and her other friends told her that she needed to take it easy. With her previous experience with pregnancies and the included stress of losing Lance, they had ordered her to practically be on bedrest. She was relieved from chores at the boarding house, and was ordered to relax and take gentle walks. Lianne felt like a loose end.

Richard didn't make her feel like a loose end. He allowed her to come onto his land and while there were some initial protests, he let her do some light chores around his house. He accompanied her on walks, and would sit with her on his back porch. Often, they would be in silence, Lianne reading or dozing while Richard did some carving or reading of his own. He was very good company for that.

When they did talk, Lianne found he wasn't dismissive of her thoughts of topics that shouldn't have been on a woman's mind. Lance had done that a lot, but Richard didn't ignore her. He listened, and they would end up talking for hours. Lianne was happy to have found someone to have a genuine conversation with and she didn't need to censor herself for Society's sake.

Leaving him at the end of the day wasn't easy. Even with Richard walking her back to the boarding house and making sure she got inside without any problems, Lianne didn't want to leave his side. It was a strange sensation, but she couldn't help it.

It should have been dismissed immediately. She had only just found out that she was a widow. Her husband was barely cold in the grave, and here she was finding her comfort in another man. She should have stopped it from the outset. But Lianne couldn't bring herself to do so.

Lianne was still thinking it on the way back from a walk with Richard, leaning on his arm, when there was another sharp pain in her side. She bit back the wince of pain and tried to keep walking, but the pain made her sway. Richard grabbed her as she tipped sideways.

"Lianne? Are you all right?"

She wasn't, but Lianne wasn't about to say anything. She didn't want Richard to worry. That would have her worried, and she knew she needed to just take deep breaths. Afterall, the twinges had been going on for some weeks now and controlled breathing had sorted it out then. Though, they were getting more intense, but she was managing.

Even if they made her want to burst into tears.

"I'm fine." She managed to give Richard a smile. "It's nothing, really."

Richard snorted in disbelief.

"Nothing? You've been doing that a lot lately."

"The baby's just wriggling around a lot." Lianne rubbed her belly, hoping it would ease the twinge. It did, but not much. "I guess I'm rather sensitive to it all right now."

Normally, Richard didn't argue with her. Her pregnancy was one subject where he backed down. But this time he gathered her in his arms and led her briskly over to the back porch. They had only been walking across the back yard -- the furthest Lianne could go right now -- but it felt like a long way away.

"What are you doing?"

"You need to sit down."

Lianne groaned.

"Don't start now, Richard. Everyone is treating me like I'm an invalid right now."

"After what you've been through, I'm not surprised," Richard muttered back.

He sat her down in a chair that Richard had brought out specially for Lianne to use. Then he knelt before her, snagging the blanket and tucking it around her lap. Lianne could only watch him as he tucked the blanket into the chair, his hands gentle as he looked after her. It was a contrast to the gruff man she had first met.

Richard Baxendale had certainly softened a lot in the last couple of weeks. Lianne wasn't sure what to make of it.

Richard eased back on his haunches. Then he realized Lianne was looking at him.

"Why are you looking at me like that?"

"I'm trying to figure out if the man before me is the same man I approached two weeks ago."

"I'm afraid so." Richard's cheeks went red. "You've made me soft."

"Is that such a bad thing?"

"I don't get my emotions involved. Far too messy."

Lianne could understand that. Richard had told her before with Beatrice, his first love, he had worn his heart on his sleeve. After her betrayal and turning her back on him, he closed up and kept to himself. It wasn't that difficult to see why he was the way he was. But it did make her want to hug him.

"Were you a loner in the army as well?" she asked.

Richard settled back and leaned against the porch post. It seemed to be his favorite spot during their talks.

"Pretty much. I kept to myself. Especially after...you know." He cleared his throat. "Being a tracker meant I could be out on my own. I didn't need to interact or speak to anyone unless I absolutely had to."

"And now I've turned all that upside-down."

"Essentially."

Was he trying to make her feel guilty? Lianne did feel a little guilty, but she also felt proud that she was able to draw the man out. He had been a brusque man, but he was just hiding his pain. He wasn't as strong as he made himself out to be.

Lianne wished he didn't have to do that.

"Do you miss being in the army, Richard?"

Richard was silent. He looked out at the back yard.

"Sometimes," he replied after a moment. "But there are days when I'm relieved. You see things...it's not pleasant. And it haunts you. You can't get away from it."

"You have nightmares?" Lianne sat up. "You see things even when you're awake and you believe you're back on the frontline?"

"Yes..." Richard blinked at her in confusion. "How did you know?"

"My father was a soldier. He suffers from it as well." Lianne grimaced as she remembered the memories. Finding her father in the middle of a waking nightmare on numerous occasions had been terrifying. "Mother was the only one who could keep him on an even keel. The nightmares for him eased when she was around."

"She was a calming influence on him."

"Yes." Lianne reached out and touched his shoulder. His body tensed, but Lianne didn't pull away. "You remember when you said to me that you were there if I needed someone to talk to? It goes both ways."

Richard stared at her. Then he smiled. One of the

few genuine smiles that Lianne had seen from him. It made her feel warm inside.

Richard laid his hand over hers.

"Just having you here is making me feel better. Just don't make me admit that too often."

Lianne giggled.

"I can't promise anything. But I'll do my best."

CHAPTER SIX

"*A*re you sure you don't want me to walk you back?" Richard asked for the fifth time as he and Lianne reached the gate.

Lianne sighed. He had been hovering over her like a mother hen ever since she nearly keeled over walking earlier. It was sweet, but also very annoying.

"It's fine, Richard. Really," she insisted when she saw Richard's skeptical expression. "It's still light. I'm not an invalid."

"You're heavily pregnant, though." Richard pointed out. "Anything could happen."

"I'm not in the army, and what is going to happen?

You think someone is going to jump out and attack me?"

"It could happen."

Lianne laughed and prodded him in the chest.

"Since when have you been so protective over me?" she demanded. "Not that I don't like it, but it's not like you at all."

Richard said nothing. Then he took Lianne's hand, pressing a kiss to the back of her knuckles. His eyes never left Lianne's, and she could see them darkening. It was enough to make her catch her breath.

"I've been protective of you since you walked into my life." Richard's reply was soft. Almost territorial. "You know how to make sure I can't let go."

For a moment, Lianne forgot how to talk. This was the closest she had ever got to Richard admitting anything close to his heart. Emotions for him were not easy to come by. So, to get that...

Lianne licked her lips, aware that Richard's eyes were now on her mouth.

"I'll take that as a declaration of something," she croaked.

Richard's mouth twitched in a small smile.

"That's as close as you're ever going to get to me." Leaning over, he kissed her forehead. "Now, off you go before I change my mind about letting you go alone."

After a declaration like that, Lianne didn't want to leave. But she knew it would be far too scandalous to stay. She was already treading a line by spending too much time with Richard. That part she didn't care about, but any further than that would be tempting fate she didn't want.

She needed to leave right now, whether she wanted to or not.

It wasn't too far to the boarding house from Richard's cabin. A little further than Lianne could manage alone, but she would be able to go straight to bed as soon as she stepped in the door. Beth was always hassling her to her room, making her rest as much as possible. Lianne wasn't sure if Beth or herself was more worried about the baby.

Lianne shuddered to think what Beth would be like once she was about to have her own baby. Her poor husband, whoever that may be.

She was barely at the end of the street when someone stepped out of the shadows. Lianne barely gave them a glance, simply a nod in their direction before stepping around them. But the shadow stepped with her and grabbed her arms.

"Where is she, Mrs. Colebrook?"

Lianne gasped as his fingers dug into her arms. That hurt.

"Let me go!"

"Where is she?" She was shaken hard. "Tell me!"

That was when Lianne saw him. A very large man, one that she had known for some years as a neighbor. She had hoped never to see him again.

"Mr. Platts? What are you doing here?"

"What do you think?" Adrian growled. He grabbed her hair, tugging her head back hard. "You're going to talk to me, Mrs. Colebrook. Where's my son?"

His son. Lianne should have guessed Adrian Platts

wouldn't let this go without a fight. No matter what anyone else wanted, Adrian Platts had to be in control. His son was terrified of him and wanted to get away as fast as possible. Lianne could understand that, and that was why she had managed to convince him to come to Sioux Falls. She had made a solemn promise not to say a word.

And she was sticking to it.

"I don't know," she hissed back and tried to tug away. "Now, let me go."

"Not a chance. You're going to tell me exactly where that woman is who kidnapped my boy. And then you're going to show me."

Lianne began to panic. There was no question about what Adrian would do once he found them. With a cry, she kicked out and connected her foot with his shin. Adrian yelled and his hold loosened. Lianne drove a knee into his stomach and then tried to run. Only to have her skirts grabbed by Adrian, who hauled her back.

"You're going to pay for that," he snarled as he slapped her. "You little chit."

CHAPTER SEVEN

*R*ichard hadn't thought he would ever find a woman to touch his heart, not after what happened to Beatrice. He had kept them at arm's length, not willing to be broken again. And yet Lianne had managed to squeeze past his defenses. It was unnerving how easily she had accomplished it.

But Richard couldn't bring himself to complain. Having Lianne around was not as strange as he thought it would be. He liked having her with him. He liked it a lot, even if it wasn't a good idea. She was a pregnant widow. That was cause for scandal. Then again, their first meeting hadn't exactly been conventional.

He should have walked away a long time ago. He didn't need to hang around her. But Richard just...he just couldn't.

A banging at the door, followed by a heavy thud, had Richard jerking out of his chair by the fire. Grabbing his gun, he ran to the door and flung it open, only to have Lianne sag into his arms.

"Lianne! What...?"

"Help me," Lianne pleaded weakly. She cried out and sagged to the floor, clutching at her belly. "The baby's coming. I can feel it."

"The..."

Then Richard saw the blood. It was staining her skirts, and was spotted along the porch. In the firelight, Lianne was pale and sweating. In the five minutes since she had left, things had changed. It was all too fast.

It was then that Richard saw the red finger marks on her cheek.

"What happened?"

"I was attacked," Lianne gasped. "Adrian Platts...he

wanted to know where his son was. And I... I wouldn't tell him. Then he..."

It was then that she stopped talking, gritting her teeth as she screamed. Her hand clamped hard onto Richard's arm, her nails digging through the cloth. Richard was not experienced in childbirth, but he wasn't stupid. Lianne was having contractions.

Lifting her into his arms, Richard carried her over to the couch and laid her down, propping her head up on the cushions.

"Just stay there and breathe. I'm going to get James Waters."

"*No!*" Lianne grabbed his wrist with a strength Richard didn't realize she had. "You can't! I'm going to have this baby at any moment. And I don't want to be alone."

"I'm not a doctor."

"But Mrs. Mason lives opposite. She's closer." Lianne grimaced and spoke through gritted teeth. "Get her, please!"

"Only if you let me go."

It took a moment, but Lianne's grip loosened. Richard pulled away, only to hesitate and go back to her. He pressed a kiss on her lips, stroking her hair off her clammy forehead.

"I'll be as quick as I can," he promised.

He ran out of the house and across the street. He knew Martha Mason. She was an experienced midwife and caring mother. While they didn't interact much, Martha was always giving him a nod of greeting and the children gave him a wave.

Richard could only hope that she was in as he pounded on her front door. Moments later, the door opened and Martha was there. Richard had never felt so relieved to see someone.

"Mr. Baxendale?" Martha stared up at him. "Whatever's the matter?"

"I need your help." Richard panted. He was starting to feel dizzy. "Mrs. Colebrook has just been attacked and she's now in labor."

The change in Martha was immediate. She became a different woman, tossing the cloth in her hands aside and grabbing a bag that sat near the door.

"Where is she?"

"At my house. I didn't know what to do."

"Don't fret. I've got it." Martha turned as her eldest son appeared behind her. "Charlie, go to Doctor Waters and tell him a woman's in labor. Go!"

Charlie darted out the door and ran down the road. Martha grabbed Richard's arm and urged him into motion, herding him towards his house. Lianne was still on the couch when they entered, curled up in a fetal position. The sounds of pain coming from her were awful to hear.

"Mrs. Colebrook?" Martha put the bag on the floor and knelt beside her. "Mrs. Colebrook, it's Martha Mason."

"It hurts," Lianne whimpered. She sounded close to tears. "It really hurts."

Richard hovered in the background as Martha did her checks over Lianne. He felt useless. Lianne was in pain, and all he wanted to do was to get rid of the pain. But he couldn't. It made Richard want to run the other way, but he forced himself to stay still. Lianne didn't need a coward right now; she needed someone with her.

He wasn't about to run from that.

"All right." Martha had brought out a small pocket watch and had been timing the contractions. She put it away in her bag. "Your contractions are less than three minutes apart. You're definitely in labor. If they keep going like this, your baby will be here in no time."

"I never thought it would hurt this much," Lianne whimpered.

Martha smiled.

"You won't remember the pain once your baby's here. Now, I'm going to need you to sit on the floor. I'll fetch some blankets for you to sit on, but it will be a lot easier if you're upright."

"I'll get some blankets."

Eager for something to do, Richard charged through the house and found as many blankets as he could. By the time he got back to the living room, Martha had managed to get Lianne onto the floor and sitting on some cushions. Lianne was going through another contraction, her face contorted in pain.

"Thank you, Richard." Martha took the blankets off him and laid them beside her. "I'm going to need you to help me here now."

"Of course."

"Sit down behind Lianne and let her lean on you," Martha instructed. "Hold her hand and support her. Don't let go."

Richard wasn't planning to. He settled down between the couch and Lianne, whereupon Lianne immediately leaned against him. She was shaking.

"I'm scared," she whispered.

"I know." Richard kissed her hand, slipping his hand into hers. "I've got you. I'm not going anywhere."

CHAPTER EIGHT

*R*ichard stared in wonder at the baby sleeping in his arms. He had never witnessed anything like it. Lianne had done a splendid job, fighting through the contractions even as the pain nearly became unbearable. But Martha had talked her through everything, keeping her as calm as she could. And soon baby Rose had been born, shortly before James arrived.

Rose certainly had a healthy pair of lungs. But as soon as Lianne fed her and they had skin-on-skin contact, she settled right down. Now Richard was cuddling a swaddled baby while Lianne and Martha were alone, Martha checking Lianne over and cleaning her up, and Richard and James were in the kitchen tending to Rose.

Or, rather, Richard was holding Rose, unable to let go.

"Richard?" James was looking at him expectantly. "You're going to need to let go of her. I can't examine her if you're holding her."

"Sorry." Richard was reluctant to let her go. But he handed Rose across to James. "I just couldn't let go."

James smiled.

"I noticed. But I'm going to need to check her over, just to make sure she's well. Would you mind helping me?"

"I'll do what I can." Richard shrugged. "After all, I managed to help Lianne through labor. This seems like a walk in the park."

James laughed.

"I'll remember that."

James' checks didn't take long. Rose stirred a little and wriggled as James made sure there were no limbs missing and no sudden bleeding from anywhere. He checked that the umbilical cord had been sufficiently tied off before checking her ears, nose and mouth and her temperature. When it was time to put the cloth diaper on, James was looking at it apprehensively. Richard laughed.

"You don't like doing those?"

"I admit, I do find them a little difficult to manage."

"Give it here."

Richard took the diaper and a safety pin. In less than twenty seconds, he had Rose wrapped up in both the diaper and in the blanket. She had gone back to sleep, snuggling into Richard's arms as he picked her up.

Then Richard realized James was looking at him oddly.

"What?"

"Are you sure you're not a father yourself?"

"No, never had the pleasure. Why?"

"Because you're a natural. She's very calm with you."

Richard shrugged, leaning on the edge of the kitchen table.

"I was the eldest of twelve children. Someone had to look after the others while Mother was giving birth or laid up afterwards."

Much as he loved his siblings, Richard was glad he didn't have to do that anymore.

There was a knock at the back door. Keith was there, taking off his Stetson as he hovered in the doorway.

"Can I come in?"

"Sure." Richard felt a swell of pride in his chest as he displayed Rose to his friend. "Come meet Rose Colebrook."

Keith took one look at Rose and he completely softened. He bent over the sleeping baby and stroked her head.

"Hey, little lady. You had us scared for a moment, do you know that?"

James laughed as he packed away his things into his bag.

"I think this is the only time I see men going gooey, and it's all over a baby."

Keith flushed and stepped back. Richard adjusted his grip on Rose. She stirred and stretched before settling back down, her eyelashes brushing against her cheeks as they fluttered.

"Any word on Adrian Platts?" Richard asked.

Keith shook his head.

"Afraid not. He's vanished. But if he's injured, he won't get far."

"It's unlikely I'll be treating him, anyway." James snorted. "Not after what he did."

Richard didn't think anyone would be helping Platts. Word would be all around Sioux Falls by morning with what he had done. Lianne had managed to tell him between contractions that she had got in a few hits of her own, but Platts had attacked her when she refused to tell him where his son was. It had brought on the early labor.

It was only by a miracle that Rose was healthy in spite of being over a month early.

"Don't, Richard."

Richard looked up to see Keith giving him a stern look.

"I wasn't doing anything."

"I know what you were thinking." Keith shook his head. "You want to go after him."

"Of course, I do. Wouldn't you if it had been Simone? He could have killed Lianne and Rose."

"But he didn't. Lianne is alive, and so is her daughter." Keith indicated the sleeping baby. "You focus on them. Let me do my job."

Richard didn't want to. He wanted to find Platts and tear his throat out. But Keith was right; Lianne and Rose needed him more. If they allowed him around.

He would step back. For now. But not for long.

CHAPTER NINE

*L*ianne settled onto the couch, wincing
before the comfort kicked in. Her hips were
propped up on clean cushions, as well as
behind her back. It was uncomfortable, but it was
worth it.

She had never expected it to be so painful. The
others had mentioned that childbirth would be tough
and it would come with some pain, but they had still
made it sound like it was the easiest thing in the
world. Lianne wasn't sure about that. She had cried
through the pain, wanting to suck the baby back up
and run away.

But now Rose was here, and Lianne couldn't wait
to cuddle her again. James and Richard had taken

her into the kitchen to check her over while Martha looked after Lianne. The midwife had been a saint throughout it all, barely batting an eyelid at anything. She didn't even look ruffled when Lianne kicked out in her direction, simply carrying on as if nothing had happened. She was a godsend.

The room had been cleaned up. There was no longer any indication that someone had just given birth on the floor. Martha folded away the bloody blankets and smiled at Lianne.

"Better now?"

"Much better." Lianne gave her a smile. She was exhausted, but she just couldn't stop smiling. "Thank you, Martha."

"Not a problem." Martha picked up the bloody towels and stood. "I'll fetch you a strong cup of tea. Plenty of sugar. You're going to need to get your sugar levels up."

"All right." Lianne wouldn't complain about that. "What about my baby?"

"Doctor Waters will more than likely be finished

giving her a check-up." Martha looked up as the door opened. "Here they are now."

Lianne looked up. Richard was walking into the room, holding Rose in his arms. The sight of him holding a baby had Lianne wanting to cry. It looked like the most natural thing in the world for him to do. It was such a homely vision.

Richard smiled at her.

"Ready for a little visitor?"

"Please." Lianne held out her arms, and Richard passed her daughter over. Lianne looked down at her sleeping daughter, unable to believe this was her little girl. "Hello, Rose. You're back with Mama now."

"I'll leave you to it while I sort out that tea." Martha squeezed Richard's arm. "Take care of her."

"I plan to."

Martha left, closing the door behind her. Richard managed to perch himself on the edge of the couch. He had some blood on his shirt, but he didn't seem to notice. He stroked Rose's head.

"She's healthy. James is happy with her."

"I'm glad." Lianne could feel a tear trickling down her cheek. She wiped it away. "Thank you."

"No need to thank me." Richard's hand moved from Rose to Lianne, brushing another tear away with his thumb. "You did all the hard work. I just tried not to get my fingers broken."

Lianne laughed.

"Sorry about that."

"It's fine. I don't use that hand much anyway."

"Silly fool." Lianne nuzzled his palm as Richard cupped her jaw. "You were there when I needed someone, Richard. You could have just thrown me out on the street."

"I wasn't about to do that." Richard shook his head. "God help me, but I wouldn't have been able to walk away."

His hand slid through her hair, cupping the back of her head. Then he was kissing her, the barest brush of lips. Lianne sighed and leaned into him, kissing him back. It was only when Rose squeaked and squirmed that she remembered there was a baby between them. She drew back.

"Sorry. I forgot where I was."

"I think I did as well." Richard then kissed Rose's head before drawing back. "What would you say if you and Rose stayed here? Just to make sure you have someone to keep an eye on you. Someone to take Rose while you rested."

Lianne stared. He was offering her a home? Didn't he realize the implications of that?

"You do realize people will talk if I move in," she pointed out. "I don't want that to happen..."

Richard laid a finger over her mouth.

"I did think about that. I mean, Rose needs a father. And I want you around a bit more permanently than you are right now."

It took a moment for Lianne to figure out what he had just said. In his roundabout way, he had just offered her something that Lianne had never expected to be given again.

"You mean...we...we get married?"

"Yes." Richard shrugged. "This seems to be the best option."

"You do make it sound very clinical, Richard."

Richard took her hand and lifted it to his mouth, kissing her fingers. His eyes never left hers.

"You know this is anything but clinical, Lianne," He replied softly. "And you know how hard it is for me to admit anything involving the heart."

Lianne did know. And she knew Richard. His actions, his brisk words, they said everything to her. Smiling, she squeezed his hand.

"Then let me say it for you. I love you." She tugged him closer. "And the answer's yes."

CHAPTER TEN

*A*nother match. Another wedding. James felt a sense of pride as he sat back in his chair and watched Lianne and Richard together. They hadn't wanted a big wedding -- Richard was still not keen on crowds -- so they had got married in Richard's backyard with just a few close friends present. It was small, but it was warm and inviting.

Lianne looked stunning for someone who had given birth two weeks before. She had taken to motherhood perfectly, and James couldn't find any fault with her. Rose was a lively, bubbly baby and she melted everyone's hearts. She had certainly melted Richard's, and the man was very protective towards her.

The tracker's heart had been well and truly melted.

There was one slight blot on the occasion. Adrian Platts. He was still around. Even after two weeks, there was no sign of him. There had been blood at the place where he had attacked Lianne, but because of Lianne's early labor it was hard to tell if any of the blood was his. He had gone to ground. No one had seen him. If they had, they weren't giving him up.

James couldn't think why anyone would hole him up. The man had attacked a pregnant woman. Lianne and Rose could have *died*. Thankfully, they had made it and Rose was healthy. It could just as easily have gone the other way.

Platts would have a lot to answer for. He was a stranger to Sioux Falls, so it shouldn't have taken this long to find him. Yet, he had managed to slip away.

But James was more concerned about what Platts had said to Lianne. He was looking for his son and the woman who had kidnapped him. He seemed to think Lianne knew where they were.

James had a feeling Lianne did know. And, in the pit of his stomach, he knew as well. There was only one person left that it could be.

And Frederica hadn't been accounted for by Keith and his deputies. Because she was holed up in James' house with Colin. The two of them were terrified, refusing to leave the guest room except for food. James felt pained whenever he walked past the door. It was not fair they were living in fear.

But why were they running? And what was this about a kidnapping? James had tried to get answers out of Frederica, but she always diverted the conversation.

Hopefully, not anymore. But James was going to need some help.

Keith was nearby with Simone. His stepson, Luke, was talking to him and Keith was giving him a proud smile, one that a father would give a son. James stood and braced himself. This wasn't going to be easy. The sheriff was not going to be pleased.

Keith saw him coming and excused himself from his wife. He met James halfway. From the expression on his face, he knew exactly what James was going to say.

"Are you going to tell me where Frederica is now,

Doctor Waters?" he asked. "Or am I going to arrest you for obstruction?"

James winced.

"They made me promise to keep them hidden, Keith. And I wasn't about to break that promise."

Keith stared at him. He snorted and shook his head.

"How far would you go for that woman?"

"What's that got to do with anything?"

"You've matched all the other women who came here with you apart from her. I didn't think you'd match yourself."

James growled.

"That's not funny."

"It wasn't meant to be." Keith sighed. "I need to talk to her, James. Now. And I won't have any stalling."

James knew that. He was already tempting everything by not disclosing anything to the sheriff. He beckoned the man to follow him.

"Come this way."

Read on for a preview of the next exciting book The Bride on the Run

Frederica felt a pang of regret as she heard the church bells ring. She had wanted to go to Lianne's wedding and see her marry Richard. She wanted to get more time to coddle Rose; the child absolutely melted her heart. But she couldn't. Not while Platts was still around.

It was frightening that nobody knew where he was. Frederica didn't want to contemplate what would happen if she went to her friend's wedding and Platts managed to find her. She couldn't see anyone else hurt because of her. Lianne and Rose could have *died* because of Platts' actions before.

Hopefully, Frederica could see her friend the next day. Lianne had suggested that she come over the day after and spend some time with her before she and Richard settled into parenthood. They were going to delay their honeymoon until Rose was older. Lianne didn't seem too upset about it, and Richard simply shrugged about it. Frederica loved their laidback attitude and how relaxed they were around each other. Frederica could only hope she could have that for herself one day.

That wasn't happening while Platts was still roaming around, though. She couldn't go anywhere; Frederica was stuck with Colin in James Waters' guesthouse behind the surgery. It wasn't a palace, but it did well for them and James looked after them. He was staunch in keeping them safe, not bothering with asking too many questions.

He would, eventually. Frederica was just hoping things would be cleared up before it happened.

"Frederica."

Frederica looked up. Colin had been reading perched on the window seat. Now he was sitting up and looking out the window. Frederica wished he wouldn't do that; Platts could easily find them that way if he was passing by.

"What is it?"

"Doctor Waters is coming this way," Colin hissed. "And he's got the sheriff with him."

This wasn't good. Frederica jumped to her feet, tossing her sewing aside.

"Get away from the window and go into the bedroom," she said, hurrying over to the boy and urging him off the window seat. "Quickly."

"But..."

"No buts. *Go!*"

Colin didn't argue further. He hurried into the bedroom they shared and closed the door. Heart hammering, Frederica approached the door just as a firm knock sounded, one she had heard many times. Before she answered, she checked her hair, making sure nothing was out of place.

This was ridiculous. Frederica had been fawning over her appearance far too many times since coming to Sioux Falls. Never had she done it before. It was the doctor, it had to be. He had her all done up in knots.

Bracing herself, Frederica opened the door. James was standing on the porch, Sheriff Keith Dickinson behind him. But Frederica could barely keep her eyes off James. Tall, blond and handsome, James Waters casted a fine figure. Frederica had been captivated with the sight of him when she first met him at the train station, on the way to go to Sioux Falls. That had been very unnerving, something she had never experienced before.

His kindness and sweet nature toward her didn't help matters. Frederica could feel her defenses falling away every time he was around.

Aware that she was openly staring at him, Frederica turned her attention to the sheriff, who wore a grim expression.

"Sheriff. I didn't realize I was getting an escort to Lianne's wedding," she said lightly. "She knew I wasn't able to make it."

"This isn't an escort, Miss Parkin," Keith said. He didn't even smile. "We want answers."

Answers? Frederica looked at James for help. His expressions usually said everything. James laid a hand on her arm.

"Can we come in, Frederica?" he asked gently. With that soft tone of his, he could get her to do anything. But Frederica hesitated.

"I'm not sure if I should let you."

James said nothing. He simply looked at her. They couldn't stand on the threshold like this, and from the way he was tensing up, Keith looked like he was close to barging in. Frederica stepped aside and let the two men in, closing the door behind them. This was not going to go very well.

She turned to Keith, who had taken off his Stetson and was turning the brim around in his hands.

"Are you going to arrest me?" she asked.

"For what?"

"I..." Frederica faltered. "I don't know."

They stared at each other. The tension was getting thick. Frederica had a sudden feeling like she wanted to run away. James stepped between them, raising his hands to make them stand down.

"Let's take a step back, Sheriff." He turned to Frederica with a pained expression. "Listen,

Frederica, we know you're the one Platts is after. We just don't know why. You will need to start at the beginning."

"It's because he wants me back."

Frederica jumped. Colin had come out of the bedroom, standing just within the main room with a defiant tilt of his chin, glaring at both men as if he was daring them to argue. James faltered. Even Keith was looking startled.

"What are you saying, lad?"

"My father wants me back." Colin moved to stand beside Frederica, slipping his hand into hers. "And I won't go with him."

"You're his son?" Keith stared at Frederica. "You kidnapped him from his father?"

"No!"

"Frederica didn't kidnap me," Colin said sharply. "Mother told her to take care of me."

"Whoa, let's slow down here." James held up a hand to stop Keith from launching into an onslaught of questions. "We're jumping too far ahead here." Then he held out the same hand to Frederica. "Frederica? Why don't you sit down and start at the beginning?"

Frederica wasn't so sure if she should. He was asking her to tell them everything, the reason why she had agreed to join them on their move to Sioux Falls. Frederica was so used to being quiet about it for so long that she wasn't sure that she could bring herself to relive it. But she slipped her hand into James' and allowed him to walk her over to the chair by the fireplace. His fingers were warm around hers. Frederica didn't want to let go.

James urged her to sit and then he settled on a stool beside her. Colin hovered near the window while Keith stood in front of the fireplace, arms folded, a dark scowl covering his face. Frederica stared at her hand in James' grasp. He hadn't let her go.

"I was Mrs. Platts' maid. She was a very sweet lady. But she also confided in me that her husband was abusive, that he would sometimes hit her and Colin. But now Colin is growing up, and he was soon going to be able to fight back. Mrs. Platts was scared that Mr. Platts would kill Colin for standing up to him. So, she told me to get Colin away and look after him if anything happened to her."

James and Keith exchanged glances.

"She believed she wouldn't last long?" James asked.

Frederica shook her head.

"She was a strong woman, but in the last three months she was in her bed more than out of it. She was so sickly; it is a wonder that she had made it that long. Mrs. Platts would have a few days of being well and going back to her normal self, and then she was back in bed."

Keith's frown deepened.

"You sound as though you suspect foul play," he said.

The Bride on the Run will be out 13th May click here to join my newsletter and to get a reminder.

The Hands and Hearts Mail Order Bride Agency Series:

The First Bride

The Bride who Stole his Heart

A Bride for the Faithful Groom

The Pregnant Brides Trouble

The Bride who Ran Away

A Love to Last a Lifetime Series novel length books:

The Second Chance Bride

The Love in His Heart

The Arms of a Better Man

Santa Fe Brides and the Rescued Animals Books 1 to 3

Santa Fe Brides and the Rescued Animals Books 4 to 6

Santa Fe Brides and the Rescued Animals Books 7-10

31 Sweet Brides – a massive Box Set of sweet romance

If you would like to find more of our books look on our Amazon page

Indiana Wake was born in Denver Colorado where she learned to love the outdoors and horses. At the age of eleven, her parents moved to the United Kingdom to follow her father's career.

It was a strange and foreign new world and it took a while for her to settle down. Her mom raised horses and Indiana soon learned to ride. She would often escape on horseback imagining she was back in the Wild West. As well as horses, Indiana escaped into fiction and dreamed of all the friends she had left behind.

From an early age, she loved stories. They were always sweet and clean and more often than not, included horses, cowboys and most importantly of all a happy ever after. As she got older, she would often be found making up her own stories and would tell them to anyone who would listen.

As she grew up, she continued to write but marriage

and a job stole some of her dreams. Then one day she was discussing with a friend at church, how hard it was to get sweet and clean fiction. Though very shy about her writing Indiana agreed to share one of her stories. That friend loved the story and suggested she publish it on Amazon Kindle. Together they worked really hard and the rest, as they say, is history.

Indiana has had multiple number one bestsellers and now makes her living from her writing. She believes she was truly blessed to be given this opportunity and thanks each and every one of her readers for making her dream come true.

Follow Indiana on Amazon https://www.amazon.com/Indiana-Wake/e/B00YHFIIJY

Follow Indiana on Facebook https://www.facebook.com/IndianaWake/

Join Indiana's Newsletter http://eepurl.com/dn6ogf

Thank you so much for reading this book. I love to write and to share my stories with you and hearing your wonderful comments gives me great pleasure. Until our next adventure keep well my friend xx

Made in the USA
Middletown, DE
16 July 2019